TITAN ISLAND:
TRIALS AND TREPIDATION

ISBN: 979-8-9887977-0-8

Illustrations by Uriah L. Crawford and Dixie Strain

Interior art by Canva Pro

Printed in the United States of America.

TITAN ISLAND:
TRIALS AND TREPIDATION

URIAH L. CRAWFORD

PROLOGUE

The boy had no clue what ocean he was drifting on, how he got there, and whether he would end up dying in it. He felt weak, scared, and fragile. His bones ached with every sway of the small raft as it floated across the waves. Although he had no thoughts on his location, his mind was in so many places, and imagining so many things at once, he couldn't think straight. He'd been desperately searching for land, food, and freshwater for the past four days. There used to be a small fishing rod in the boat, but it was tossed overboard by strong waves.

Every day was spent trying to remember how he got here. But what made this odd, and more difficult, was the fact that he could not remember anything. Not even his name.

"I'm so hungry," he moaned.

He directed his gaze to what he guessed to be the night sky; it was so dark. An array of magenta and pink streaks flashed unpredictably overhead. Every time the light flashed, it illuminated the shrouded canopy. It was beautiful and frightening at the same time. This phenomenon scared him even more than he felt it should have. It wasn't even the fact that this whole situation was extremely out of place—it just made him feel so vulnerable. It was unsettling. He eventually dozed off, hungry and scared.

The next morning, he assumed he would die knowing he was starved out of his mind. His body rocked as he bobbed along the deep blue ocean. He continued to scan the horizon desperately in search of land and food despite his hope sinking faster than his stomach.

An abrupt jerk backward snatched the boy's attention. He quickly looked around to see what caused this, then peered down at the water below. Small shiny fish sped through the water. He shifted his gaze to see where the fish were coming from.

What he saw made his heart freeze.

A giant blue wall barreled towards him.

"Tsunami," he gasped.

He wasn't sure how this unfamiliar word slipped from his lips, but he got the feeling that a tsunami wasn't a good thing. He began to paddle furiously despite how weak he was, so much so that, if he went any further, it felt like his arms would fall off.

But he didn't stop.

He was too terrified to stop.

The rushing of the monster behind him roared in his head. He slowly turned and saw the massive wave only yards away. He frantically looked in every direction in search of escape but when he turned around, the water struck.

Before he knew it, he felt squeezed and his ears began to pop. The tug of the wave pulled him along as he fought back and his lungs began to burn. He was pushed under with such force and ferocity he thought he would die from that alone. The wave pulled him behind itself, dragging him across the current into a coral reef with massive branches protruding from the rocks. He narrowly missed the branches until a large green fish swam out of a rock in front of him. He covered his face to shield his head. When he removed his hands he saw a white branch of coral right in front of him. He then felt a sharp pain shoot through his body and everything went dark.

He slowly, so slowly lifted his eyelids and was immediately blinded by the sun. He felt warm sand between his toes and the gentle waves lapping over his legs. He was on land, a beach. He felt a thrill of happiness but was too exhausted to celebrate. As he began to feel his body again, he felt a lot of sharp things poking him. He reached under him and picked up a small odd shell. His ears were ringing but eventually, he steadily sat up.

Shells that ranged from the size of a marble to a cow scattered across the sand. None of them were identical. They all had random black stripes and pink ovals plastered onto their creamy white bodies. He could barely move and had a pulsating headache throbbing inside his skull. It didn't matter though; he was on land, and he needed food.

CHAPTER 1:
SHELL-SHOCKED

He was so hungry and tired he didn't have the patience to think of an effective way to find food. He ravaged the beach, picking up shells and looking inside them. He dug in the sand and even traversed through the shallow tide in search of food. He lifted rocks and peeked inside holes, finding nothing. But he knew there had to be something.

After moving back to land, he kept searching until he finally found a broken, fuzzy yellow shell inside a bush near the outskirts of the trees. Whatever was in it had escaped. The boy grunted in anger and continued to search.

He found himself inside a cave near the beach scrounging through it for food. The formation of the cave didn't seem natural. The corridors seemed too perfect to be real. Almost like something purposefully created them. He got about 100 steps into the cave when he entered a wide area. "Hello?" He called. He listened to the solemn echo of his voice. A soft light shone on an area of the floor. He looked up and noticed a small hole that opened to the sky but it was overcast, so only a dim light passed through.

He examined the walls and floor for food. As he searched, he realized that everything was covered with deep, jagged lacerations that seemed like scratches. Then it came together. This room—the whole cave—had been carved out by something. Something big. Just as this realization hit him the clouds passed over the sun and bright light filtered through the hole in the ceiling. It took some time for his eyes to adjust. When they did, he was left dumbfounded when he saw mounds upon mounds of more fuzzy yellow balls, some three times the size of the one he saw on the beach. But in the center of it all was what really made the boy dizzy. In the middle of the mounds was an enormous hermit crab.

The animal was starting to emit a strobing neon-green light and had the same kind of shell as the ones outside. It was truly massive. Luckily, it seemed to be sleeping and didn't notice him. The boy stood there staring at the crab, mesmerized. This hulking monster was so frightening that it convinced him, despite his hunger, to leave the cave and search for food somewhere else. He turned slowly, eager to sprint, but decided to creep slowly instead, knowing that this was the best course of action. He made it five steps before feeling a sudden crunch under his right foot. He had stepped on one of the balls. The fragile ball shattered, letting a small blue animal ooze out.

It was an egg.

They were all eggs, and the crab must have been the mother. The sharp crack of the egg echoed all over the

walls sending chills down his spine. The beast began to vibrate and flicker an eerie light. The boy slowly backed up, hoping it was dreaming or something. It raised its antennas, twirling them, seemingly sensing the disturbance, then followed with its eyes.

Those eyes. The gaze of the eyes pierced the boy's soul. They were boiling pink, elongated pearls with occasional bursts of aqua shooting through them. They absorbed his train of thought, leaving him petrified. It was then the massive crustacean laid its sickening eyes on him. Its gaze switched from the egg to the boy, then the boy to the egg until it finally marked him as a threat. It rose to its legs and opened its horrifying maxillipeds, moving every little part in different directions until they stopped abruptly and the creature let out the most ear-splitting cry the boy had ever heard. The sound demolished his hearing and exploded off the walls. His ears began to bleed and his head was ringing painfully.

He needed to escape.

He turned and ran the way he came as fast as he could, which wasn't very fast as he was extremely malnourished. He got halfway out before feeling enormous crashes through the tunnel. He turned and saw a bright light aggressively flashing different colors in the hall.

He didn't stop, knowing that the entrance had to be close. He ran for a little bit more and dashed out of the mouth of the cave. He bolted to a nearby bush and hid. The crab followed and immediately began searching for him across the vast beach. He was terrified; he was in some messed up world with no food or people and now some crazy monster was hunting him. He waited, unaware of where the crab was at that moment. He tried to stay quiet but the sprinting took a lot of energy from him. It took a lot to conceal his breathing. It had now been 10 minutes. He continued to wait until eventually, he heard something.

Click, Click, Click, Click, Click.

An antenna brushed his neck. He slowly turned his head and saw the giant crab. He busted through the bush but got his right leg stuck in the twisted twigs. The crab took this chance to grab his right leg with its smaller claw. The boy kicked it twice with his left leg, freeing himself. He got out of the bush and hobbled as fast as he could towards the forest.

The crab thundered after him, demolishing trees and leaving destruction behind it. He leaped over glowing roots and ducked under branches. He ran until his run slowly became a jog as he began to become weak and tired. The crab saw this and began to run faster until it was only a few feet from the boy. It reached out its smaller claw trying to grab him. The thundering of each leg as it stomped after the boy became louder as it got closer. The crab extended a little bit more until it was only inches from the boy. But, right before it could grab him, he heard a loud snapping sound and then whistling coming from the left. The boy and the crab looked up and saw a small brown ball shoot through the trees. The crab shrieked as it broke into its shell. The crab was blown on its side and it writhed on the ground. At first, all that could be heard was the screaming crab. When suddenly, there was a faint sizzling sound coming from the shell. It got louder and louder until...

CRACK!

The crab's shell erupted in a cloud of embers and heat. The boy ducked to avoid pieces of shell. The crab let out a cry of anguish as it squirmed on the ground. The boy didn't know what happened but he was too scared to care. He turned and dashed away.

The boy eventually found a clearing and ran behind a rock near the tree line. He peeked around it, realizing how beautiful it was. It had tall trees and stunning flowers. It also had scaly cow-like animals eating the grass. They had skin like elephants, horns and feet like rhinos, and tails like alligators. They looked scary but seemed quite passive, yet the boy didn't know for sure, so he never let his guard down. He was so amazed by the beautiful landscape and the sweet aroma of the flowers that he was put in somewhat of a trance. He was in a feeling of peaceful tranquility. He felt he could look at it all day when suddenly...

BOOM!

The crab came crashing in, screeching as it did, rattling the trees. Half of its shell was gone, and smoke rose from its back. All the cow-like creatures let out low bellows and trotted for the forest across from the crab as the boy held his ears.

But they unexpectedly came running back. The boy was confused as to why they would run back toward danger. But he got the feeling that his question would be answered soon when thundering footsteps began to shake the trees in the area they came from. The quaking crashes got closer and closer until the trees opposite the crab were uprooted and crashed down in the grass, sending a cloud of dust around them. The boy watched the cloud with terror and curiosity. Even the crab seemed curious. The suspense was abruptly snapped as a colossal *something* emerged out of the cloud. It was an enormous red reptilian creature with jagged teeth, midnight black skin, two huge legs, and patches of purple feathers on its body. It was roughly three times the size of the crab!

The sight paralyzed him. The creature spotted the crab and stopped. It let out a huge, deep roar and charged. The crab, although clearly out-matched, tried to charge at the creature, too.

It didn't win.

The lizard grabbed the crab's eyes in its jaws and swung it around. It slammed it on the ground, killing it instantly. The lizard roared triumphantly over the dead crab and gruesomely bit its head off, swallowing it in one gulp and then dragging the rest back into the forest.

This was when the boy realized that his life will

not

be

easy.

CHAPTER 2:
AN ENEMY IS MADE

The boy felt...small.

He felt like he could be killed at any moment. Whatever world he was in, whatever huge island he was standing on, seemed out of place, and it scared him. The purple night sky lit by constant lightning, giant hermit crabs, and lizards; it was just too much for him. He didn't even know why or how he got here. His whole body trembled uncontrollably, and the thoughts of giant monsters eating him alive screamed in his brain. He whimpered as tears formed in his eyes, and he began to cry. The tears streamed down his face. He continued to cry until he noticed a faint sound coming from the clearing. He wiped his face and lifted his head to look over the rock. What he saw filled him with so much joy, he felt he would pass out. It was a stream. It was a stream of crystal clear water. His mouth began to water and his fingers twitched. He started for the stream when he suddenly stopped. He knew that he could be killed at any moment. He wasn't sure whether he should go or not, but he needed the water. He pushed back his fear and surveyed the land.

When he felt it was safe, he emerged from his hiding

place and ran as fast as he could toward the stream. When he arrived, he slipped his hands in the stream and felt the cool water lap over his arms. He cupped his hands and brought the water to his lips. It smelled of citrus and glittered like diamonds. He sipped the water to get a taste. It had a weird sweetness to it that he liked, not like the bitter saltiness of the ocean's water. One sip turned to two, and then three, and once a handful was gone, he shoved his hands in for more. He drank, and drank some more. He drank until he was startled when he saw something moving in the stream. He assumed it was a fish; it squirmed and glinted in the sun like a fish. It dove deeper and disappeared, then suddenly it shot up, jumping out of the water.

The fish was enormous, with large fins and a sleek, platinum body. It was about the length of his arm span and had a large round mouth. As it was in the air, it suddenly gulped in a huge amount of air and inflated itself, then it closed its mouth, started flapping its fins, and slowly floated into the air towards what seemed like a shiny cloud. But on closer examination, the cloud seemed to be moving. Apparently, it wasn't a cloud at all, it was more flying fish. The sight left the boy in awe. It was so odd, and yet so beautiful.

But his thoughts were interrupted by the angry growling of his empty stomach. He needed to find food. Just as he thought this, he saw a twisted black tree with strange red fruits. At this point, he didn't care what it looked like, as long as he could eat it. He walked to the tree and stood on a rock to reach a fruit. He bit into it, hoping it wouldn't kill him.

"This is…this is…*amazing*!" The fruit tasted sweet and hydrating. He couldn't stop eating it. He ate so much that he thought he was going to burst. He finally felt renewed and replenished. Now he could focus on something else: building a camp.

He couldn't just run around vulnerable to giant creatures; he needed a safe house. Somewhere to hide and stay safe from predators. He thought about finding a cave to live in, but after the crab incident, he ruled that option out. He sat on a fallen tree as a winged rodent scurried out of the trunk squeaking in anger as it took off. He began to consider his options. He thought about building a treehouse, but he had no carpentry skills, at least none that he could remember. Finally, he came to a decision: he would try to live near a clearing in the forest. The trees would provide protection while the clearing itself would provide an escape from the tangled vines and crossing roots, there would also be many resources, and many animals to eat because he couldn›t live on fruit forever. With this plan, he started for the forest. However, when he reached the treeline he froze. He was suddenly petrified as his mind raced with all of the possible ways he could die. Shredded by lizards, swallowed by plants, pecked to death by scaly birds, he didn't know what could happen. "No!" he scolded himself "You can't do this. Being scared won't help you survive." He shook his head and held it high, refusing to cower in fear. He swallowed his terror and stomped to the trees.

He traversed through the warped landscape of cobalt blue trees and neon-orange moss until he discovered a marshy area with dead trees and green standing water. The swampy location had a hazy fog draped over the ground and it gave him an eerie sensation, one of which sent shivers down his frail spine. The light barely permeated the thick canopy of leaves and only slightly revealed light in the dark, black area. At first, he was reluctant to enter the green liquid, but he knew that getting across it was his only choice. The water was shallow enough that he would see any aquatic threats swimming up to him instead of going around the huge area, which could lead to more dangers than he could ever imagine.

He took one step in the water and trembled at its cold, wet touch. When he let it engulf his lower half, he winced at the feeling of algae and plant tendrils brushing his legs. Then he slowly began to power through the marsh. He went a short distance before hearing something reverberate through the trees around the swamp. It was a deep, ominous growl.

"Hey!" he called, feeling a sudden burst of confidence.

But this boost quickly faded as he heard it again. That deep trembling growl, and this time it was closer. He strode faster now, eager to escape this sound. He strode about ten more steps until suddenly his left foot plunged into a hole in the swamp bed. He thrashed around furiously, but when he looked down, he saw his

foot was entangled in thick, luminescent vines. After about a minute more of aggressive wiggling, he heard a deep earth-shaking stomp, and another, and another after that. They were getting closer.

Boom, boom, boom.

They continued, faster and faster until it was a full-on run as the creature began to splash through the marsh.

Boom, boom, boom, boom, boom, boom, boom, boom, boom, boom.

Until they stopped.

The marsh was suddenly quiet and still. The boy was frozen in the middle of the swamp. A glowing bug slowly flew around his head. He followed its blinking lights until it landed.

The boy felt lightheaded. The bug's light revealed something so terrible and frightening, he thought he would puke. In the faint glow, the boy saw two piercing, fire-orange eyes staring back at him. The creature stepped forward into a small beam of light emerging from the leaves above. The boy could see it more clearly now, almost perfectly, and it was a dreadful sight.

It was a reptile-like creature of gargantuan proportions with a lime-green frill emerging from its head. It had pale blue scales with streaks of burning orange striping on its sides, and green speckles. The monster reeked a stench that engulfed it like a toxic gas. The boy could only describe this cold presence as evil, pure evil. The reptile bared its teeth, revealing a set of jagged jaws ready to tear flesh with a single bite. Its breath smelled of blood and ash, and was tainted with its victims' fear.

This monster was very thin and it was drooling like it hadn't eaten in days, ready to swallow the boy whole. The creature opened its mouth and frilled as it let out a heart-stopping, skull-shattering roar. It was so loud, the trees around him seemed to bend and twist from its power. When it brought its head back down it looked the boy in the eye one more time before reopening its mouth, wider than ever before, and lunged at the boy. The boy could do nothing, he was stuck, weak, and petrified. He thought about how far he had come just to die by a giant lizard.

But right before it swallowed him whole, he heard the faint whistle of something overhead. An arrow struck the monster right in its right eye. The lizard fell to the ground, salivating and writhing. The boy saw a burning rage in his eye, a rage that could only be quenched by the death of whatever shot him. This all was too much for the boy, and suddenly everything went dark.

CHAPTER 3:
BATTLE BUDDY

When the boy opened his eyes, he was being dragged across the ground by firm, worn-out hands. He couldn't fully see, but he could make out that a human figure was towing him.

He heard the buzz of life thriving through the forest. His head was ringing painfully, and his muscles ached. He barely noticed the fact that another survivor was with him now. He heard a shriek that sounded like agony mixed with a yearning for vengeance. The figure pulled him faster now.

But the boy was way too exhausted and dizzy, so he fell asleep again.

When he awoke, he was welcomed with a warm sensation. He found himself in a room lit by a fire in the center. He slowly scanned the room for the person who saved his life.

"Welcome to the mystical world of Titanus."

The boy heard the voice behind him and jumped in fright. The boy regained himself and turned around. "Hello," the boy said, "is that the name of the island?"

"Nope! It's the name of the whole archipelago! This is just the mainland, Titan Island." The boy shook his head remembering the question he should have asked first. "Sorry, sir, but did you save me?"

"Yes, I did! Twice, actually!" replied the man. The boy stared at him, confused. "Oh, the other time was with the crab. You know, the whole explosion thing? That was me." the man clarified. The boy didn't even realize that he was saved twice.

"Thank you..." the boy paused as he didn't know the man's name.

"Oh the name is Redrick, but you may call me Red. You are?" He stepped closer to the boy, revealing his face in the dancing flames. He was a thin, gangly man with dirty, greasy hair and twisted yellow teeth, and he had ugly bruises and scars marking his body. The boy was entranced by his appearance. "Do you have a name?" Red asked again, waiting for an answer.

"Oh, ummm…" The boy thought quickly. "My name is..." Redrick leaned in. The boy eventually shrugged. "I don't know my name." He dropped his head.

"No worries, I'll name you. Your name is...Nova."
"Nova?"

"Yes! It means, 'new'. You know, because you are new here." Red clarified.

He thought about it for a little bit. "Okay, I like it. I guess my name is Nova."

Just then, the ceiling started shaking from massive, explosive stomps and screams of rage. "Ummm...are we underground?" Nova asked.

"Yes!" Red replied triumphantly. "I dug it out myself."

He started rambling on about the structure of his dugout with great enthusiasm, but Nova wasn't paying attention to him as much as he was paying attention to the scratching he heard at the trapdoor.

Red must've noticed his concern because he stopped rambling and asked him how close he came with the trepidon.

"Trepidon?" Nova echoed.

"Yes, that big lizard?" Red started walking over to a corner of the room. "Do you think I wasn't supposed to name those monsters?" He scoffed. "Oh, and the dinosaur thing you saw earlier was a colossalisk and the crab was a megapod."

"Wait, have you been following me?" Nova asked

"Yep! Ever since you washed up on the beach. How else would I have saved you twice?"

"Good point." Nova replied.

Red walked over to a hidden hole in the wall and pulled out a recurve bow with luminescent arrows that had colossalisk feathers on the end. Nova was astonished by the skill Red must have to even get close enough to a colossalisk for a single feather, let alone dozens. The scratching at the door was getting louder.

"How close did you get to the trepidon?" Red asked with a sudden sense of urgency.

"About a foot. Why?"

"Get behind the couch. Now!" He pulled Nova behind a carved stone in the shape of a couch.

"What is it?" Nova asked worriedly.

"He tracked you," Red whispered. "I'm not quite sure why he is after us, but I do know that he is using your scent to track us."

Light began to filter through the lacerations in the wooden trapdoor. The trepidon was almost in. It let out a loud, ear-shredding roar. Red pulled back the bow and aimed it toward the trapdoor, ready to fire. The scratching suddenly stopped. There was a long, silent pause that felt like an eternity. The only sound was the creaking of Red's bow. Nova reached to his left and grabbed a rock. He tried to muster all the courage he had to fight so he would not be dead weight to Red. Nova trembled in silence, anticipating when it would end.

Everything was still until, suddenly, the trapdoor crashed open and caved in, releasing the monstrous creature.

The trepidon's right eye was now mauled and swollen with massive bubbles that oozed green pus. It roared as it lunged into the hole. Nova and Red dodged it at the last second so it slammed its head into the ground. It shrieked and veered up on its hind legs before trying to slam Nova with its body. It narrowly missed him but came crashing down and reduced the stone couch to rubble.

Nova and Red scrambled to the ground outside the hole. "I can't get a shot!" Red cried.

Nova was terrified but he wanted to do something to help. He looked down at the rock in his hand and then at the mauled eye of the trepidon. He reeled his arm back, released the rock, and watched it sail toward the

trepidon. But he missed. He watched the rock fly toward the trepidon, bounce off its arm, and hit the ground. The trepidon looked down at the rock, slowly raised its head, glaring at Nova, and bore its teeth as its frill opened. It roared and leaped at them with its claws outstretched. Nova looked up at the monster flying towards them. Nova screamed, and ducked with his hands over his head. He was screaming when he heard a whistle and then a thunderous groan as something struck the ground.

Nova looked up confused. He saw the trepidon on the ground thrashing in pain, wincing and whimpering. Red had shot an arrow and it struck the trepidon in the eye, making it erupt in green slime. The trepidon thrashed for another short period of time before slowing down and closing its eyes. "Is...he dead?" Nova asked between gasping breaths. When he didn't hear a reply, he looked around confused. He saw Red going towards the forest and jogged to catch up.

CHAPTER 4:
A LASTING CONNECTION

"Red?" Nova said when he caught up. "Can you teach me how to defend myself?"

Red was silent.

"Please? I need to learn how to defend myself to survive."

"No, you aren't ready."

"But—"

"You aren't ready because you need to learn to think. You almost got us killed back there. You threw a rock at a trepidon without thinking about the fact that a pebble wouldn't hurt a giant lizard. All it did was make it mad. The trepidon species are an *evil* species. They are mindless killing machines and will find the slightest reason to justify gruesomely torturing another animal. You know nothing about this world. When you prove yourself, then we can talk about training. I can't let you die, not again."

Nova paused. *Again.* The word lingered in his mind. *What happened?*

They were traversing through the dense forest area of the island in search of a clearing to camp near, since Red's home was destroyed. The forest might as well have been breathing; it was so alive. There was a buzz of life in every tree. Nova tripped on some long worm, making him run into a neon tree trunk, sending sparking beetles and winged lizards scattering through the leaves.

"Keep this up and you will kill yourself before a monster can." Red scoffed as a smirk slipped through.

"Haha, very funny, Red."

They continued to move through the forest. At one point, they found a herd of the plant-eating cow-lizard creatures.

"Hey, what are those?" Nova asked.

"I call those 'buffalords', and they make good food!" Red jumped around excitedly. "I haven't eaten in two days!" He quickly pulled back his recurve bow and fired a luminescent arrow. It flawlessly pierced through a buffalord's heart, and the creature let out a deep groan before slamming to the ground. Red sprinted to the animal and pulled out a knife, immediately sawing off one of the hind legs. Without attempting to cook it, he sunk his yellow teeth into the leg, blood trickling down his chin. If he did care about eating raw meat, he didn't show it as he offered Nova the other back leg.

Nova turned around and puked all over the ground. When he finally calmed and turned back to Red, he grimaced. "I'll wait to cook it."

"Ok, suit yourself!" Red said, holding onto the leg for later. He tied the leg over his shoulder and they started off.

They traveled a little more before they finally found a clearing. "Time to build camp!" Red announced. Red went down the list of the things they needed. "We need branches from a plank tree and pelts from a carpetback." As Nova was about to open his mouth, Red cut him off. "Let me finish. A plank tree has branches that are perfect for shelter because they are flat and as strong as titanium, but also relatively light." He sighed and scratched the side of his head in thought. "And like I said, we also need the pelts of a couple of carpetbacks."

"And wh—" Nova started as he was cut off again by Red.

"A carpetback is an armored reptile creature that resembles a turtle and sleeps halfway underground with its shell above ground. They are called carpetbacks because they sleep so much that their backs are eventually covered in moss and make good blankets."

"Sounds easy enough. Let me take them!"

"Not quite." Red shook his head. "When awake, they aren't very lazy." He lifted his shirt and pointed to a nasty scar on his side. "Their beaks are knives."

Nova kept trying. "Come on, you're an old man, I can take them."

But Red wasn't budging and sent him to get the branches.

On the way to the plank tree, Nova kicked every pebble he came across. "He will never let me show him what I can do," he grunted. He glanced at the map Red gave him to locate the tree. It indicated about one hundred steps further. "You're too new…you're too weak…you're not ready," Nova mumbled to himself. When he finally got to the spot he pulled out the wooden hatchet Red gave him because he "wasn't ready for a stone hatchet".

The plank trees around him were stunning. They were brilliant shades of emerald with enormous masses of branches, each covered with glowing aqua leaves. The forest also had a mystical vapor floating around it. He climbed up a tree that was isolated from the others and started hacking on the branches. He struck the bulb connecting the branch to the trunk as Red said that part wasn't strong. He hit the branch many times, causing it to fall off, and moved to the next. "I wonder how Red is doing?"

Just as he said this he heard the rustlings of plants behind him. He glanced over his shoulder, feeling suddenly on edge. "Maybe it was just the wind." He continued to hack. He hit the next branch twice more before he heard the leaves again. He jumped out of the tree, hatchet in hand. This time he was sure it wasn't the wind "Whatever you are, show yourself!" he yelled, banging the tree to make noise. His eyes darted back and forth searching for the disturbance. "I said show yo—"

BAM!

"Ow!" Nova rubbed his head and looked up at the tree behind him. The branch he was hacking had fallen on him. After he realized what happened, he turned around and saw something. Something that made his toes curl and his throat dry.

Seven lizard creatures were baring their fangs at him. They held an uncanny resemblance to the trepidon, just a lot smaller. They had jagged claws, long tails, and the aura of evil. The same awful presence as the trepidon. It made him sweat and his heart choke.

Nova held up his hatchet with a trembling hand. "It's okay, Nova, now is your time to prove you are capable of surviving," he reassured himself.

They began to circle him. They hissed and slurped their wet tongues in and out. One jumped at him with an unhinged jaw, but Nova knocked it to the ground. "Yeah, take that!" Then another jumped at him from behind, knocking him to the ground. He rolled across the dirt, narrowly avoiding its snapping jaws. It pinned him and tried to bite him. Nova put his hatchet in its mouth to hold him back. It drooled pink saliva on his chest. The saliva was hot and it made him gag. He was so disgusted that he thought he couldn't go on, but the glint of its sharp teeth snapped him back. He held it back a little longer until it broke the hatchet with its jaws. "Oh, great."

It snapped again, but Nova dodged it and rolled from under the lizard. He ran, stumbling over tails and dodging leaping jaws, and scrambled up the tree. "Red, help!" he yelled, repeatedly, desperately. He began to cry. "I'm not ready and now I'll be eaten alive because of it."

Then Nova heard something. He wiped his eyes and looked up. It sounded like a shout.

"Alaaleeauhhhaeeaaualll!"

There it was again, closer this time.

Just then, Red came crashing through the trees, shouting and waving his glimmering hatchet around. He charged after one of the lizards and in a flash, he sliced one's throat. Blood sprayed in the air past a light beam slicing through the trees. It glimmered a sparkling red light. The lizard fell to the floor with a thud thrashing around until it couldn't anymore.

The other lizards jumped back, making whining sounds, and they retreated to the trees.

Red just single-handedly stopped that whole clan of reptiles with such speed and capability. I couldn't even scratch them. Maybe I'm not as ready as I thought I was, Nova thought.

There was a pause. "Are you okay...Nova?"

"Y-Yeah, I'm fine."

Red helped him down. "Those were trepidiles...the trepidon's minions. The trepidon is still trying to kill us; he is still alive."

"How is that possible? Red, didn't you kill it? Red!?"

"I DON'T KNOW!" Red snapped. "I-I don't know." Red squeezed his fists.

There was silence.

"Red, I'm sorry, I shouldn't have gone off like that, I'm just scared."

"It's fine Nova...I'm scared, too."

"Maybe I'm not as ready as I thought I was," Nova admitted.

"No, you aren't," Red agreed. "But it's my job to get

you ready."

Nova looked up. "Are you saying what I think you are saying?"

"We start training tomorrow." Red smiled.

CHAPTER 5: WARRIOR TRAINING

When they returned to the clearing, they built a small hut by strategically propping the branches on a sturdy tree. The hut had enough space for two and there were two entrances on either side. Red went to sleep as Nova lit a fire and roasted his buffalord leg.

It was amazing.

"Gosh, it's been a while since I've eaten good meat!" The tender and juicy meat was irresistible and the sweet, but savory taste made Nova's brain melt. He savored every bit. After he had licked his fingertips and cleaned the bone, he joined Red on the carpetback blankets to sleep.

The next morning, Nova was thrown out of the tent and jolted awake by the poking of pebbles on the ground. "Hey, wake up!" The man yelled. "Geez, you sleep like a rock! I thought you were dead!" Red wiped the sweat off his forehead. "Do you want to train or sleep!?"

Nova was reluctant, as he was still sleepy, but he really wanted to train so he stretched and slowly stood.

"So, first, you need to learn the hatchet." Red handed him a freshly carved hatchet as they walked toward a tree. The hatchet had a wooden handle from a neon-green

tree and a newly polished, very sharp rock on the end. "Hit the tree until it falls," he ordered.

Nova nodded and took the hatchet. He raised the weapon, with much struggle, and swung it at the tree. It didn't even leave a scratch. He swung again, and still, nothing. "This is going to take a while," Nova chuckled nervously.

"Yep!" Red agreed. "I'll check on you when you're done!" He waved and went back to the hut.

Nova went back to chopping with a slight feeling of regret. He was sure that he would be able to cut this tree down, but he also knew it would take a while. He still wanted to train, but he didn't like *this*. Either way, it had to get done, so he kept swinging.

After a few more hours, Nova was sweating immensely. It kept dripping into his eyes and his grip on the handle was slippery. The tree now wobbled from Nova's hits and the trunk started to make cracking noises. It continued to shake until eventually...

CRASH!

The tree hit the ground and Nova joined it.

"I'm done!" He shouted, exhausted. He hoped he was done, but something told him he was far from it.

"Okay!" Red called back. He came running out of the new hut with another recurve bow, just a little smaller. "I made it last night!" he proudly announced. "Now, here." He handed Nova the bow and a few arrows. "Shoot those." He pointed toward eight targets made of woven dark green vines from the marshy swamp. "I made them while you slept! Have fun!" Nova raised the bow and once again, Red went to the tent and left him to figure it out alone.

"Some teacher," Nova scoffed. He nocked an arrow to the bow and aimed it at a target. He pulled it back as far as he could and released it.

It only went three feet.

Nova sighed and fired again. It went farther...by one inch. Nova nocked, pulled, and fired again...and again, and again, missing every shot until eventually his fingers let go of the arrow and the arrow wobbled through the air, hitting a target. Barely.

"Yes!" He shouted to no one but himself. "Only seven more to go." He looked around at the targets and sighed. "I'm not sleeping tonight."

« « «

"I'm never going to hit these stupid targets!" Nova exclaimed. He had hit only one other target since the first. He now felt disappointed, as it was only getting harder. He called Red over to complain. "Why is it only getting harder?"

"It's only getting harder because you aren't strong enough yet."

"How can I get stronger?"

"It will take days, maybe even weeks, and we never

know when the trepidon could launch an attack. We should hold off on bow practice. But," Red kindly took the bow back, 'I do have something else." He ran to the tent, then quickly returned with another weapon.

"This will be your best one. Over my years of being here, I have been running from these behemoths with no way to kill them quickly at long range. I had my bow, but it takes a good bit of skill, like aim and power, and, when you are on the run, you may not have time for that." Red lifted the ammo cartridge and rotated the weapon as he spoke. "But with this invention of mine, you can shoot much faster because it can be preloaded. You also don't have to worry about aiming because it shoots large projectiles at high speed. I call it an 'arm cannon'; it straps on your forearm and you can load it with things like rocks, big berries, or animal droppings! It doubles as a weapon and a distractor." He thrust the weapon forward and mimicked blasting noises. Nova couldn't help but smile.

"These vines attached to sticks are fastened onto a band. When you pull back the ammo, the vine attaches to the band, holding the ammo back. Then you pull this latch to fire," Red said as he pointed to a latch. He gave Nova the arm cannon and a crimson bag of rocks for ammunition.

"That's not a rock," Nova said, noticing an odd, brown sphere in the pile.

"It's not, it's a flame seed."

"Flame seed?" Nova echoed, confused.

"Yes, it's a nut that explodes on contact. It's what I used to save you from the megapod."

"Wow," Nova said with astonishment. Before he could ask any more questions, Red walked off to the hut. "Oh, I almost forgot. You have to shoot those wooden targets!" Red called back over his shoulder.

"Okay!"

Over on the tree line, there were some wooden dummies in the shape of the trepidon's face that Red salvaged from his former home. Nova admired the craftsmanship of the weapon as he prepared for practice. "The old man has some pretty good skills," he chuckled. He loaded the arm cannon with a rock and cocked it. He then pointed his arm at the dummies. "Okay, let's do this, I guess," he sighed, and he pulled the trigger.

The arm cannon shot with such force that Nova fell back onto the ground. The rock shot through the trees, making a hairless orange ape chatter in anger. "*Owww! Geez!*" He stood up, rubbing his behind. He reloaded the blaster, cocked it again, and aimed it at the statue. This time, he braced himself for the blast, and this time, he hit it.

"Yes! Second try!" he whooped. The blast hit a target making it burst into thousands of splinters. "Gosh, this thing is amazing!" He braced himself again, ready for the now-familiar force of the blaster. He pulled the trigger. It flew straight at the wooden trepidon head, blowing it to shreds.

He pulled out the flame seed. "Alright, time to use

this weird thing." He loaded it into the wrist cannon, aimed, and fired. As soon as it hit the target, it stuck and started to whistle. It quickly turned red and exploded, blowing up all of the other targets around it. Splinters flew and charred the foliage where they landed.

A wave of heat blew over Nova as he ducked for cover. "Woah, awesome!" he laughed. "I think I completed *that!*" With that, he walked, chest puffed, into the hut. He could feel Red's eyes on him.

"Some kid," Red chuckled.

Nova fell asleep, feeling ready for anything.

CHAPTER 6:
THE MONSTROUS BATTLE

REEAEEAEAERRRRRR!

Nova was startled awake by a thunderous, shrieking roar that sounded all too familiar. "Red! Red! *Red!*"

He left the hut and scanned the clearing. He finally saw Red sitting on a log under a luminescent tree, sharpening his ax. "Red did you hear—" Before Nova could finish his question, Red handed him a bundle of something. "What is this?" Nova asked.

"Buffalord armor," Red replied. Nova unraveled the suit, realizing that Red was donning the same style of armor. Nova went back to the hut to put it on. As he came back out, he realized there were holsters for the bow and hatchet. He locked his new weapons in and put on his helmet.

The light glistened off the sleek plates of polished armor. He instantly felt powerful, like he could do anything. But the sensation quickly receded as another shriek boomed through the trees. "Was that—"

"Yes," Red cut him off again. "That was the trepidon. Remember, we trained for this very moment."

"Yeah, we got this."

They began to walk to the clearing where Red's last home used to be to retrieve extra flame seeds. When they got to the destroyed house, as they suspected, there was no trepidon, just a big red stain on the grass where it once was. But its stench still lingered in the air. Red went inside to get the nuts while Nova stayed above to keep watch, constantly scanning to spot any trouble.

After a short time, he heard a series of earth-shaking stomps, exploding through the forest across the clearing. "Red, hurry!"

RRRREEAEAEAEAAAEEEERRRR!

Another ear-splitting roar blew through the land. Nova saw trees falling in a path toward them across the clearing. The stomping kept growing louder and louder. "Red! Come *on!*" Nova yelled impatiently. Red finally emerged from the hole, proudly carrying six flame seeds. "Look," Nova pointed to the falling trees.

"Well alright then, let's do this." Red quickly loaded his bow. Nova loaded his arm cannon with a flame seed and pulled out his hatchet, ready to fight.

The stomping started picking up pace. The trepidon blew out every tree it touched with impossible ferocity. It continued to destroy everything in its path until it busted through the forest edge with such monumental savagery that the grass across the whole clearing bowed from the extreme force. The stench of the monster's rage blistered the land.

The trepidon scanned the clearing, searching for them. The creature was all beat up and had a nasty wound on its right eye with a huge green blister throbbing where its eye used to be. It raised its head and sniffed the air.

"Maybe it can't see as well anymore," Nova said.

"Maybe, but it still remembers your scent. The monster continued to wave its head around trying to locate them until he stopped abruptly and lowered its head as its frill began to vibrate. It bared its teeth and let out a low growl. Without hesitation, the monster charged them at top speed, careening across the clearing with no mercy.

"*Ahhhhlelelouuuoollleaall!*" Red let out his battle cry as he charged toward the creature.

It thrashed across the dry, grassy clearing, only guided by vengeance and insanity. Nova gathered all the rest of his bravery, reminding himself how far he had come. His heart pounded in his temple.

Thump-thump, thump-thump.

This was when he decided he was not going to die today.

Nova ran toward the creature with no fear. When he reached the monster, Red was already taking his chances with it, dodging and rolling through its attacks. When Red got distance from the enraged lizard, Nova called to him, "I'll distract him, you get the tail!" Red nodded and darted out of the way.

"Hey, big lizard!" It didn't work. "Nova, hurry!" Red

was still dodging attacks.

Then he remembered something. He could use the wrist blaster to distract the trepidon. He switched his flame seed ammo for a rock and launched it at the back of the trepidon's head. The stone smacked its skull, making it immediately lose interest in Red and focus on Nova.

Nova's eyes locked with the fiery ones of the lizard. He quickly loaded his arm cannon with a flame seed and fired it at the trepidon's snout. It exploded with a flurry of embers, engulfing the trepidon's face. The lizard was stunned, so Red took the chance to hit its tail, chopping off the tip. It screamed in pain and veered up on its hind legs and roared.

"His underbelly!" Red shouted.

"What?!" Nova shouted back.

"His underbelly!"

"What?!" Nova was having trouble hearing over the roaring.

"The weakest part! Shoot! The! Underbelly!"

Nova finally realized what he said. He loaded another flame seed and fired it at the underbelly, sending the trepidon collapsing on its back. The embers burned the skin on the creature's underbelly, exposing tender, red meat. The trepidon squirmed on the floor, sputtering and screeching.

Nova saw all the extreme pain and detestation plastered on its one eye. While the trepidon was still thrashing on the ground trying to get upright, Red ran up to the bubbling eye and raised his ax.

"*Alaaleeauhhhaeeaaualll!*" He screamed as he swung the ax as hard as he could, jamming it into its skull. Red grimaced as green ooze splashed and covered him.

The trepidon let out a howl of immense anguish.

Red retrieved his ax and jumped back. The lizard rolled back onto its legs, looking as enraged and mauled as ever. It looked up and roared its loudest roar yet—but this was different. The pitch fluctuated, almost like a siren. Red and Nova covered their ears. *What is he doing?!* Nova thought. The trepidon finally stopped and looked down.

After a short pause, there was the faint sound of hundreds of feet stomping through the trees behind the trepidon.

Red stood there as his ax fell to the floor.

"What is it?!" Nova asked worriedly.

"He just called his trepidiles," Red replied breathlessly.

"Come on old man, that just means he needs help and he's scared. We got this." Nova said it to sound brave, but he was just as scared as Red.

"Yeah, you're right, sorry. Let's do this." As they prepared for the worst, the sound of terror grew louder by the second. Nova and Red were ready and they stood there, waiting. The sound grew louder and louder, closer and closer, until finally hundreds of trepidiles dashed through the trees as the trepidon limped back to the treeline to recoup, glaring back at them.

"*LET'S GO!*" Red shouted and they both sprinted toward the oncoming enemy.

Red went straight through, dodging and leaping over trepidles and cutting down any in his path. Nova swiftly wove through the smaller lizards as he shot rocks at them and sliced whatever scales he saw. Nova and Red kept this up for a while until one trepidile jumped on Nova from behind and knocked him to the ground. The trepidile clamored onto his back and screeched. They all flocked toward Nova and began to pile on him; even the ones fighting Red lost interest and ran toward Nova.

Every single savage reptile piled onto Nova, gnashing their teeth. They kept biting at him, but they could not penetrate his armor. The stench was almost unbearable.

Is this it? Do I die here? No, I refuse to die here!

Nova pulled his arm away from the jaws of a trepidile and frantically loaded a flame seed into a wrist cannon and shoved it into the mass of trepidiles, closed his eyes, and fired. Instantly, a shock wave of heat and a magnificent orange light catapulted every trepidile into the air. The explosion charred the ground and killed every lizard around him. He slowly got up and rubbed his head. "Did it work?"

"Yeah I think so," Red said, chuckling as he kicked a dead trepidile. "But it's still not over. The trepidon still lives and he won't stop until we are dead."

After a brief pause, the trepidon stomped out of the trees and growled. "What, mad that you missed the party, big guy?" Red taunted.

"Don't know if that's why, but he is mad," Nova said.

The trepidon looked at the dead trepidiles and let

out an almost sad noise. But that sadness faded to rage, as it let out a thundering roar and charged toward them. The trepidon was blinded by a white-hot fury and rushed right for Nova, who had to think fast, so he ran toward it with his hatchet in hand.

They were getting closer by the second, speeding toward each other. When it got close enough the monster attempted to slice Nova with its razor-sharp claws. He barely missed, taking off Nova's right buffalord shoulder plate. Still alive, Nova rolled into a foot-forward slide with his hatchet on his stomach, facing up. He tore through its exposed flesh, making blood gush all over him. He came out behind the lizard as the monster tumbled forward. The monster rose up with an extreme struggle, and faced Nova. *When will it die?!* Nova was so exhausted that he wasn't sure he could go any longer. The monster stumbled toward him, looking him in the eye. It let out one last burst of energy and ran toward him.

"Look out!" Red yelled. But it was too late, the monster sliced his shoulder with its sharp black claws, leaving deep lacerations.

"Ahhhh!" cried Nova, falling to his knees. The monster then whipped around, striking Nova with its tail, and launching him into a nearby tree. There was a loud snap and splinters flew all around him. The breath was stripped from his lungs as he coughed up a jet of blood and crashed to the ground.

The world faded into darkness.

CHAPTER 7:
LIFE-CHANGING MEMORY

Nova woke up in a mysterious place. *W-Where am I?*

The air felt cold. A dark, empty void of nothing. His armor was gone. Instead, he wore a button-up shirt and jeans. He was clean and his hair was slicked back.

What am I wearing?

He stood up and walked around. As he walked, a white flash flooded the void and he was brought to a different place. He suddenly stood on a boat, somewhere in the open ocean.

"Hey! Want to get on the raft?" Someone called from the cockpit.

Nova heard someone call back. "I do, Dad!" Then a kid ran to the cockpit. But Nova watched in amazement, as the kid wasn't just *any* kid.

It was him.

They both came out of the cockpit with life jackets. "I want to steer!"

"Okay, Michael!"

Nova was shocked. *My name is…Michael?*

They threw out the anchor to make sure the boat didn't drift away and then the other "Nova" climbed into the raft. Just then, his dad's phone rang.

"Stay right there, I need to get this," the dad said as

he walked into the cockpit.

Michael was too excited to care that his father told him to stay put. He picked up the paddles and rowed out to sea.

"Ok, bye." His dad said as he came out and hung up.

"Alright, who is ready to ride the ra—" He stopped abruptly as he realized his son wasn't there. "Michael! Where are you!?"

Then there was a distant reply. "I'm over here, don't worry!" Michael shouted back, carefree and laughing.

"Get back here!" his dad yelled sternly.

Michael rolled his eyes and started to paddle back. On his way over, though, the wind started to blow against him and the waves made it harder to paddle. The current shifted and jerked him back. Stunned, he turned around to see what was happening and his face turned pale.

An enormous whirlpool was forming behind him.

He paddled furiously. "Help! Dad! Please!"

His dad rushed to pull up the anchor as it was still keeping the boat in place. "I'm coming son! Hold on!" His dad tried to reassure him. Michael had tears streaming down his face. He was so desperate and terrified. The whirlpool grew bigger and formed into a gaping void, churning with foaming water, roaring with the sound of the furious waves. His dad finally got the anchor up, ran to the cockpit, and hit the gas. He sped towards his son, whose raft now tilted into the

whirlpool. The sky shattered into the same flashing purple sky above the ocean that Nova was drifting upon before he washed up on the island. *This must be how I got there. It has to be*. Nova thought. Flashes of lightning, screaming winds, and crashing rain churned the once peaceful ocean into a thrashing beast. Michael's dad struggled to get to him. "Hold on, please! I can't lose you, too!" He was finally in range to throw the life ring. He went to the back of the boat and threw the ring into the widening hole.

Michael realized he had one chance. He was coming back around, but the current kept pulling him into the abyss. The raft managed to drift close enough and he extended his hand.

"Grab it! *Please*, Michael!"

Michael finally came to it. His hand ready, he reached. His fingers were barely able to brush the surface of the ring. The rushing water seemed to mute. Tears streamed down both of their faces.

Nova held his breath. Everything seemed to slow. He could feel his heart pounding. *Come on.*

He missed.

His dad's white knuckles loosened from the ring's rope and his face went pale as he watched his son get swallowed by the water.

"*Michael!*" His dad screamed through tears.

"*DAAAAAD!*" Michael's voice faded and the rapids roared as they closed.

A blinding light flashed from the hole and everything

stopped. The rain stopped, the sky turned blue, and the sea began to hum and roll gently as if nothing had happened.

CHAPTER 8:
FINISHING MOVE

Nova slowly blinked and regained his consciousness. His temple was on fire and he was pretty sure his spine was broken. He had so many questions. Why were they out there? Why did the whirlpool open?

Why did it happen to *him*?

Nova's injury was bad. He couldn't feel his legs and blood gurgled from his mouth and trickled down his chin. But, although his injury was bad, his head felt worse. He was overloaded with thoughts. He sat up against the tree he hit as he regained his mind. He heard a scream and looked up and saw Red tumble across the ground, exhausted and defeated.

The trepidon roared with triumph. Nova knew he had to do something. He jerked as he stood up and winced with every step toward the monster. But he didn't care about the pain. He had to end this nightmare. He unclipped his bow and loaded his arm cannon. He only had one rock and one arrow left. He shot the rock at the trepidon, which hit and drew its attention. When the trepidon realized that Nova wasn't dead, it was furious. The monster limped as fast as he could towards Nova, who stood his ground, drew his bow, and readied to fire.

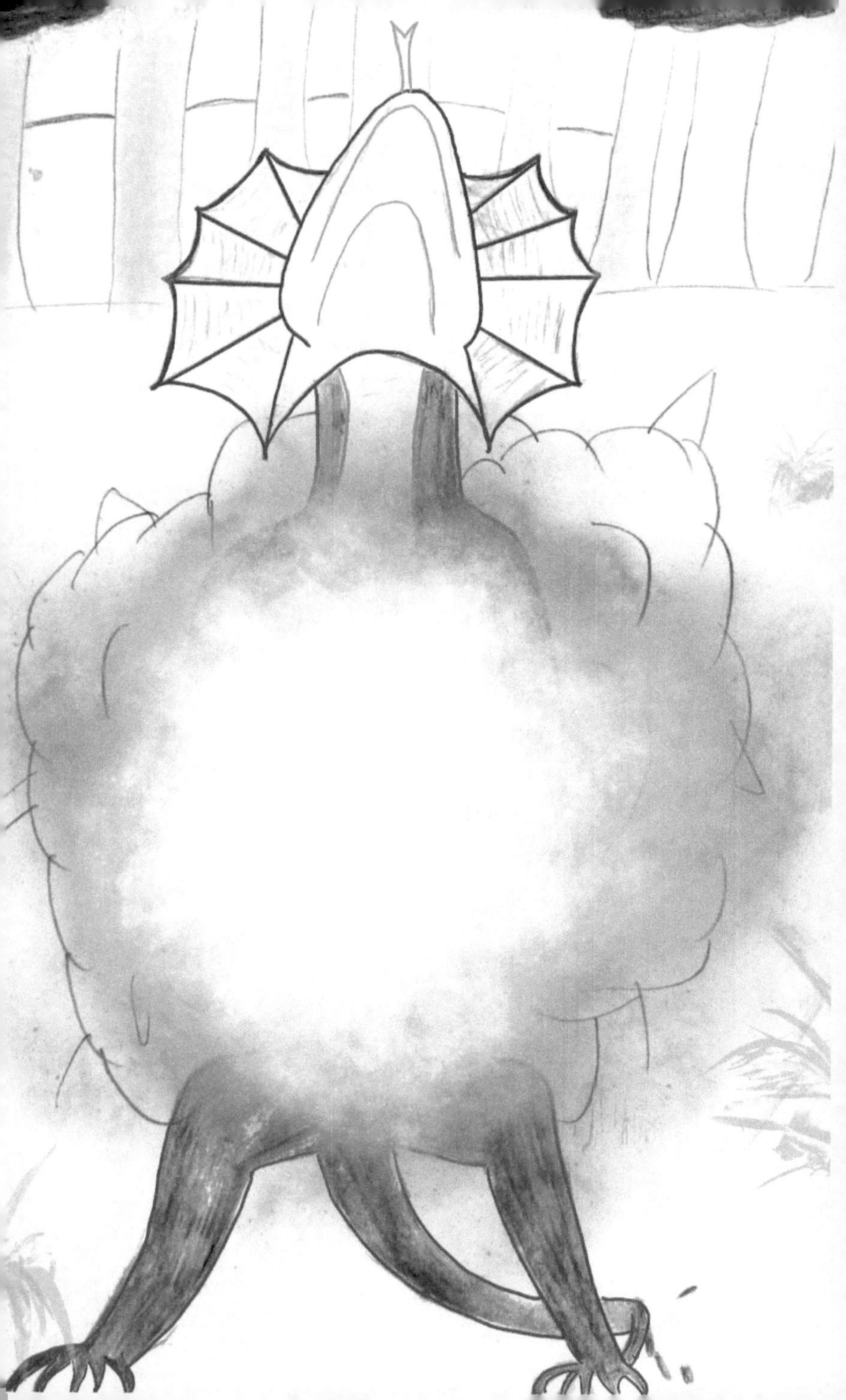

I don't really have any practice with this and my pulling arm is injured, but I don't really have a choice now, do I? It's time for this monster to die.

The lizard picked up speed, mouth open, ready to devour Nova once and for all. It roared as it ran toward Nova. He waited until the monster got into range to take the winning shot. Nova trembled as he pulled back his bow but he felt it reach full power and released.

The arrow sliced through the wind and beelined toward the trepidon, straight for the heart. When it struck, it punctured through the chest. The monster reared up on its hind legs and let out one last defeated growl before hitting the ground, dead.

Nova limped toward Red. Once he got there all he could do was collapse exhaustedly.

"We did it, buddy," Red said, struggling to sit up.

"Yeah, I know," Nova agreed. "You look terrible."

"So do you!" Joked Red, and they both laughed.

CHAPTER 9:
NEW HOME?

When they got back to their camp, Red worked on Nova's shoulder.

"Hey Red?" Nova asked.

"Yes?"

"Can I ummm...stay with you?" Nova requested nervously.

"Yeah!" Red said without hesitation.

"Really?!" Nova was surprised.

"Yes, why not?"

"Yeah, why not!" Nova agreed.

"Hey Nova, why did you fight with me? Or really, for me?" Red asked when he finished bandaging him.

"I did it because you saved my life *twice*. I mean, the only reason why the trepidon was after you was because you saved me, so I wanted to repay you," Nova answered warmly. Red smiled. "Oh, and by the way, Red, I like the name Nova."

When they finished talking, Nova left the camp to go to the beach as Red went to harvest the trepidon's carcass. He sat on the sand and admired the glistening sea. He remembered his journey there as he watched the sun shining on the water. He didn't want to tell Red about what he saw just yet. Red didn't seem dangerous, but Nova could sense that he was hiding something. Nova remembered when Red was talking about losing him and he used the word "again". He wanted to trust Red, but something just seemed off. He was still shrouded in mystery, and Nova felt that he needed to figure it out. But that thought didn't pull at Nova too hard, now that Nova knew how he got to the island, he wanted to find out if he would be able to leave and if he would ever see his family again. Just then, a shiny white bird flapped out of the forest and over the shallows of the water chirping as it did loops. Nova perked up. For now, he was content to embrace this new life and any adventure it threw at him. "So, for now, I guess Titanus is my home."

EPILOGUE

"Blast!"

"I'm sorry, I truly am, my lord. It won't happen again, I promise! Please, Lord Abaddon. If it will alleviate your anger, I have retrieved the last of the trepidon." Nefartul offered a claw with a guilty expression. Abaddon snatched it with disgust and threw it into a bubbling pool of lava.

"I don't want the remnants of a failure. I want the head of Akalum on the edge of my flaming bone blade!" Abaddon declared as he thrust his enormous sword at Nefartuls throat. "Or I shall mount your head at the top of my obsidian throne like a trophy!" Abaddon gestured up at the bloody and spiked throne that he was perched upon.

"Sir?" Nefartul choked out, "It wasn't Akalum himself that killed the trepidon."

"What do you mean, you slimy lizard?" Abaddon asked, puzzled.

"Well—" Nefartul stammered.

"SPIT IT OUT!" Abaddon bellowed impatiently.

"Akalum found another champion!" Nefartul blurted "and his name is…Nova." Nefartul saw what looked like a glimpse of terror flicker across Abaddon's face as he gingerly touched a jagged scar on his neck.

"N-no matter." Abaddon forced out. "I have a champion

of my own now." Abaddon swept one of his enormous wings over to a cave behind his throne as a pair of glowing, slitted eyes pierced the darkness. "This war will be over soon, Akalun. The dark abyss will prevail."

MEET THE AUTHOR

Uriah L. Crawford is a young man and aspiring author. He plays football and loves to hang out with his friends. As a military kid, he has traveled the world with his family and has attended many schools.

He has won many awards in school pertaining to writing and literature since 1st grade, such as an ode to the survivors of the Vietnam War. The release of *Titan Island: Trials and Trepidation* marks the beginning of the 14-year-old's path as he plans to write more books. He wants to use his words to express his ideas and talents in writing.